DISNEY
LEARNING

DISNEY
ZOOTOPIA

HOW TO BE A ZOOTOPIA POLICE OFFICER

GRIT WITH JUDY HOPPS

Jennifer Boothroyd

Lerner Publications ◆ Minneapolis

For Sara H. Thanks for the wonderful gift!

Lerner Publications Company
A division of Lerner Publishing Group, Inc.
241 First Avenue North
Minneapolis, MN 55401 USA

For reading levels and more information, look up this title at www.lernerbooks.com.

Main body text set in Mikado a 14.5/22.
Typeface provided by HVD Fonts.

Library of Congress Cataloging-in-Publication Data

Names: Boothroyd, Jennifer, 1972– author.
Title: How to be a Zootopia police officer : grit with Judy Hopps / Jennifer Boothroyd.
Description: Minneapolis : Lerner Publications, [2019] | Series: Disney great character guides | Includes bibliographical references.
Identifiers: LCCN 2018024090 (print) | LCCN 2018029178 (ebook) | ISBN 9781541543157 (eb pdf) | ISBN 9781541538986 (lb : alk. paper) | ISBN 9781541546035 (pb : alk. paper)
Subjects: LCSH: Zootopia (Motion picture)—Juvenile literature. | Police—Juvenile literature. | Police—Vocational guidance—Juvenile literature. | Disney characters—Juvenile literature.
Classification: LCC HV7922 (ebook) | LCC HV7922 .B64 2019 (print) | DDC 363.2023—dc23

LC record available at https://lccn.loc.gov/2018024090

Manufactured in the United States of America
1-45081-35908-9/6/2018

Table of Contents

The Right Candidate

So you think you have what it takes to be a top Zootopia police officer? It's a lot more than just writing speeding tickets and zooming around in a cop car! Zootopia can be a wild place. But the brave officers from the Zootopia Police Department (ZPD) are up for the job.

They work hard to keep residents of Bunnyburrow, Savanna Central, Sahara Square, Tundratown, Little Rodentia, and the Rainforest District safe.

The ZPD is always looking for skilled animals to join their team. But what skills do candidates need to get the job? They should want to help others, take on challenges, and solve problems quickly. They will have to work well with all kinds of animals, big and small.

Her Dream Career

Judy Hopps has always wanted to be a ZPD officer. She believes that anyone can be anything in Zootopia.

"I am gonna make the world a better place!" she says. Judy knows that ZPD officers make sure everyone follows the rules, so she speaks up when she sees something unfair. When Gideon the fox is bullying her friends, she stands up to him.

"Cut it out!" she tells him. Judy is already making the world a better place.

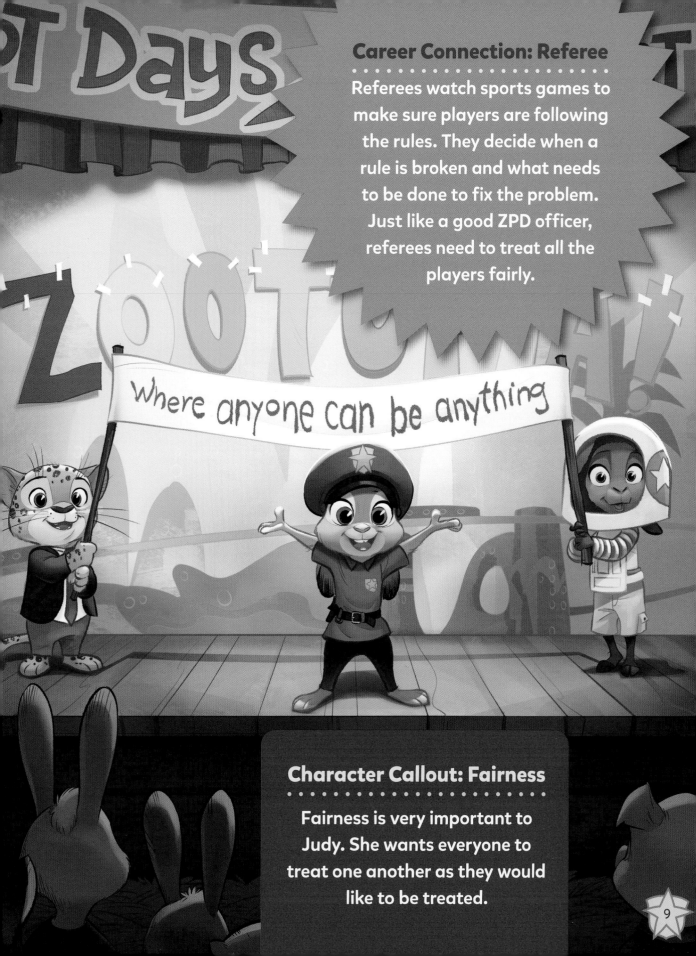

Career Connection: Referee

Referees watch sports games to make sure players are following the rules. They decide when a rule is broken and what needs to be done to fix the problem. Just like a good ZPD officer, referees need to treat all the players fairly.

Where anyone can be anything

Character Callout: Fairness

Fairness is very important to Judy. She wants everyone to treat one another as they would like to be treated.

When she gets a little older, Judy is excited to go to the Zootopia Police Academy. She's smaller than everyone else in her class, and things are hard. "Just quit and go home, fuzzy bunny," her instructor tells her.

Did You Know?
Rabbits are herbivores, which means they eat plants. Some live in holes in the ground. Many rabbits tap their foot on the ground when they sense danger.

But Judy doesn't quit. She trains harder and faces her
challenges in new and different ways. She bounces her way
to the top of the ice wall. And she uses her rabbit speed to
practice fighting bad guys. Judy finishes her training with
the best scores in the class. She becomes the first rabbit
officer in Zootopia.

On the Job

On Judy's first day, Police Chief Bogo tells the officers about missing predators. "This is priority number one," he says. He gives the rest of the officers jobs to help find the missing animals, but he gives Judy parking duty.

   She is disappointed. But Judy decides to make the best of it by doing the best she can. "I'm not going to write a hundred tickets, I'm going to write two hundred tickets!" she decides.

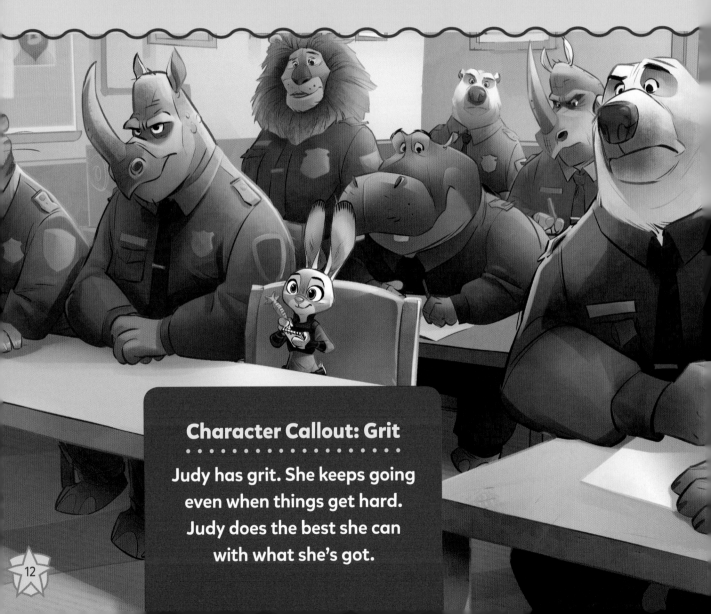

Character Callout: Grit

Judy has grit. She keeps going even when things get hard. Judy does the best she can with what she's got.

Career Connection:
Police Chief
· · · · · · · · · · ·
A police chief is in charge of
a whole police department. Just
like Chief Bogo, the chief gives
officers in the department
tasks to do. A police chief is
also in charge of making sure
officers do a good job.

13

While she is out, Judy sees a fox named Nick treated badly because he is a fox. She stands up for him. Judy still believes that everybody should be treated fairly. But then she learns that Nick tricked her and is actually running a sneaky pawpsicles scam. Judy is upset but can't do anything about it, so she goes back to parking duty.

Soon, Judy gets another chance to make the world a better place when a store owner comes up to her for help. "My shop—it was just robbed," he tells her. Judy chases the thief through the city. She's not going to let him get away!

The thief runs through Little Rodentia. Judy protects the tiny residents from harm and catches the bad guy. "I popped the weasel!" Judy shouts as she brings the thief to the police station.

Did You Know?

In *Zootopia*, each hair on every character is made separately. A mouse in Little Rodentia is covered by 400,000 tiny hairs. A giraffe in the movie has 9.2 million hairs.

But Chief Bogo isn't happy. Judy's confused. "Sir, I got the bad guy. That's my job," she says. "Your job is putting tickets on parked cars," the chief yells. But Judy wants to do real police work.

Doing a Better Job

Just then, Mrs. Otterton bursts in to ask for help. "My husband has been missing for ten days. His name is Emmitt Otterton," she says. He is one of the missing mammals. "Please, there's gotta be somebody to find my Emmitt."

Did You Know?

At first, Nick Wilde was the main character of *Zootopia* and Judy Hopps was the sidekick. The filmmakers realized that the story worked better when it was from Judy's point of view.

Judy volunteers. "I will find him," she says. The assistant mayor, a sheep named Dawn Bellwether, agrees to let Judy take the case before Chief Bogo can stop it.

Judy tracks down Nick. She's not sure she trusts him, but Judy knows he has skills to help her gather clues. "I know everybody," Nick boasts. Judy convinces him to help her solve the case.

Judy and Nick travel all over Zootopia looking for more clues. To their surprise, they make a good team. It's not easy. It's even dangerous at times. Still, they work hard and find Mr. Otterton along with the other missing animals. But the missing mammals have all gone wild. They are crawling on all fours, snarling, and snapping.

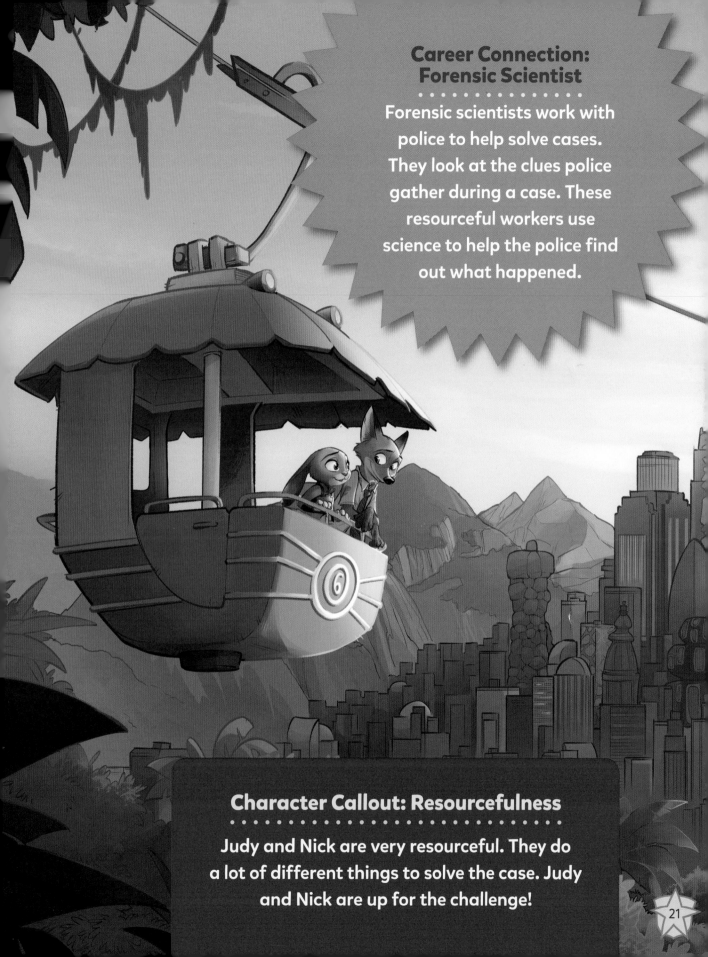

Career Connection: Forensic Scientist

Forensic scientists work with police to help solve cases. They look at the clues police gather during a case. These resourceful workers use science to help the police find out what happened.

Character Callout: Resourcefulness

Judy and Nick are very resourceful. They do a lot of different things to solve the case. Judy and Nick are up for the challenge!

Making a Difference

Judy becomes a hero. Nick isn't getting any credit because he isn't a police officer. Judy suggests that he apply for the police academy.

But when Judy is answering questions from journalists, she agrees that the wild animals may have gone back to their old ways as unruly predators. "It may have something to do with biology," she explains.

Nick isn't happy about what she's said. "Are you serious?" Nick asks her.

"I just stated the facts of the case," she replies.

Nick tells Judy that she is not as open as she thought. She is judging animals just because they are predators.

Career Connection: Journalist

Journalists write about what's happening in the world. Sometimes they travel to dangerous places or interview lots of people to find out what happened. Good journalists need to be fair and honest. They try hard to make sure they get the story right.

Judy realizes Nick has a point. She is upset that she has unfairly judged other animals. She decides to visit her family. When she returns to the farm, she is surprised to see that her parents work with Gideon now. They say that Judy taught them to keep an open mind about all animals. Judy realizes she *has* made a difference.

On top of that, Judy discovers one more clue about
the case of the missing animals! She realizes that a
special flower is what is making the animals go wild.
Judy knows she must go back to Zootopia. She needs to
fix her mistakes with the Otterton case and with Nick.

Judy leaves the farm to go find Nick. She apologizes for being a bad friend. She knows she was small-minded. "I have to fix this, but I can't do it without you," she begs. Nick forgives her, and the team gets to work.

Together, they learn that Assistant Mayor Bellwether planned the crime to make the predators go wild. They put a stop to it!

Now Judy knows what it means to be a good Zootopia police officer. She learns from her mistakes and never gives up.

Character Callout: Open-Mindedness

Judy works hard to be open-minded. She
believes that anyone can be anything. She is
open to new ideas and others' points of view
and will admit when she makes a mistake.

27

Months later, Judy is proud to speak at the Zootopia Police Academy graduation as Nick becomes a new officer. "The more we try to understand one another, the more exceptional each of us will be," she tells the crowd.

Judy and Nick are the newest partners in the Zootopia Police Department. They believe that together they can make Zootopia even better for all animals.

All in a Day's Work

Judy shows grit when she goes through the police academy, even though it is hard. How does Nick show he has grit too?

Describe a time when something was hard and made you want to give up. How did you decide to keep trying in order to succeed?

What are some ways you can help someone find their grit?

"No matter what type of animal you are, try to make the world a better place."

Glossary

academy: a school that offers special training

candidate: someone who is seeking a job

graduation: a ceremony when schooling or training is successfully completed

instructor: a teacher

predator: an animal that lives by killing and eating other animals

small-minded: not open to new ideas or the opinions of other people

To Learn More

Books
Francis, Suzanne. *The Official Disney Zootopia Handbook*. New York: Random House, 2016.
Find everything you need to be an informed resident of Zootopia.

Parkes, Elle. *Hooray for Police Officers!* Minneapolis: Lerner Publications, 2017.
Learn how police officers serve the local community.

Websites
Disney Movies: *Zootopia*
http://movies.disney.com/zootopia
Watch video clips from the movie, try out a recipe or craft, and learn more about the characters by reading their bios.

Visit Zootopia
http://visitzootopia.com/en_US
Explore everything Zootopia offers its residents. Check the weather report, and get an update from the mayor's office while you're there.